Abrogate

by Larry Gelbart

SAMUELFRENCH.COM

MUSIC USE NOTE

IMPORTANT BILLING AND CREDIT
REQUIREMENTS

CHARACTERS

THE VOICE

THE CHAIR

PROCTOR

FULSOME

JORDAN

DONE

DEBRITUS

WOMAN'S VOICE

DIAZ

CONDOLEEZZA RICE

LYNNE CHENEY

BARBARA BUSH (I)

HUGHES

THE VOICE. Good evening, and welcome to AGN, the All Gate Network, devoted to the endless scandals and excesses which White House after White House also seem so endlessly devoted to. Adding to our past retrospectives of Water, Iran-Contra, Flood and Port Gates, AGN has now assembled highlights of the recent hearings held by the special Senate committee that was charged by the present administration with the investigation of the extent to which the former administration was engaged in a campaign of secrecy and deception, as well as a thorough disdain for the law, the result of which was tantamount to a virtual second American revolution that threatened to undo the first, A nullification, no less, of over two hundred years of this nation's civil and social progress, as well as the alarming, arbitrary banishment of recognizable order or - as it has come to be known throughout and within the media - "Abrogate."

(Sound: A gavel. Crowd settling down.)

The opening of the hearings, which began the moment what had been the preceding minority became the present majority, was called to order by the venerable senator from Ohio, Senator Samuel Chippendale, the committee chair.

(Sound: A gavel.)

THE CHAIR. The chair firstly would like to apologize for the lateness of the committee's tardiness this morning, obliged as many of us were by the need to pass the body of Senator Skidmore, which was laid out on the floor of the Capitol Rotunda late last night. We have since been informed that the senator has sobered up and gone back on the program —with the pledge to cease being the obstacle he has for so long been to the work of the United States Senate. As to the business at hand, the authorization of this Committee, as anyone who cannot escape the news well knows, has been empanelled and empowered by President Hillary Clinton, so that she might better determine the following: Did the powers-that-then-were, the previous Bush administration, the pursue with both malice, and perhaps some forethought certain actions which served to violate the letters and spirit of the laws of this land in a way never herebefore thought possible? And do the sum of these reactionary actions equal a total that smacks of a conspiracy? A neoconcert of acts based upon an agenda of such egregiousness they threatened the very deconstruction of the Constitution itself? The chief question in question before this committee is, of course, what in fact if any part did the former president of the United States, consciously or possibly even less so, as was his wont, play in this ongoing accumulation of so many abrogations?

What, if any, was his role in what amounted to no less more than a mini even-quasi coup? Whatever the causes, the unavoidable fact that the American people find themselves grappling with is still one more variation of what has by now become this nation's sixty-four trillion dollar question: That is to say: what did the President know? Aside from what the Vice-President told him he already did. Let me say at the onslaught here, that I am privileged at sharing the chair of this inquiry with one of my longest standing friends, a man whose public service career cuts across the gamut from the legislative to the executive, his having previously served in the capacity of Under Secretary of Oversight. Senator Oral Proctor.

PROCTOR. Thank you, Mister Chairman. Tempting as it is to be far from honest, I am irony-bound to comment on the majority's eagerness to so readily criminalize what were priorly considered patriotic acts which, when they comprised the minority, they were always so quick to anywhere from half to wholeheartedly endorse. It never seems to fail, does it? Things always being different when the shoes are on the other foot? I daresay that if all the hearings we have so long endured teaches us nothing at all, it is that the less things change, the more they remain the same. I have nothing more to add, Mister Chairman.

THE CHAIR. My learned friend rarely does. Thank you, Senator.

PROCTOR. Only to say that I thank the Chair for his generosity in allowing me to condemn these proceedings in advance, in the event that I am called away and don't have a chance to do it later.

THE VOICE. The opening inanities dispensed with, the Chairman called as the committee's first witness, Mister Victor Fulsome, a member of the former administration and one of Washington, D.C.'s most popular and sought after witnesses.

THE CHAIR. You are Victor Fulsome?

FULSOME. *(quietly)* On the advice of counsel, I believe I'm allowed to attest to being who I am, Mister Chairman.

THE CHAIR. If the witness will please raise his right hand and his voice in that order.

THE VOICE. Victor Fulsome has a long record of governmental servitude, having assumed a great many positions under any number of lawmakers since starting as a Senate page while still in his teens.

THE CHAIR. *(fading up)* ...and nothing but the truth, so help you God?

FULSOME. So help me Him, I do, yes, sir.

THE CHAIR. Please have a seat.

PROCTOR. I thank the Chair.

THE CHAIR. I see that you are not as you otherwise indicated you might be represented here today with the actual benefit of your counsel?

FULSOME. Unhappily, he and I find ourselves in a legal gridlock, Mister Chairman, the two of us being simultaneous recipients of conflicting subpoenas.

THE CHAIR. Conflicting subpoenas being nothing to envy, I'm sure.

FULSOME. My attorney regrets any inconvenience his absence may cause the committee and has asked me, for the purpose of the record, to submit a list of interruptions which he had hoped to make had he been able to be here to make them himself, sir.

THE CHAIR. This committee welcomes all submissions. And please extend to your counsel what I know are all of our gratitude for what we can only hope will be his continued absence.

FULSOME. Thank you, Mister Chairman.

THE VOICE. Mister Fulsome's attorney, Manuelo Martinez, a former Independent Prosecutor for former Attorney General Manolo Menendez, has been summoned by present Attorney General Hernando Rodriguez to appear before Special Prosecutor Rodrigo Hernandez to answer charges of multiple counts of destruction of justice as well as a number of drug trafficking violations.

THE CHAIR. You served as a member of the prior administration, did you not, Mister Fulsome?

FULSOME. I did so, sir, in the aforementioned past, yes, sir.

THE CHAIR. An administration whose culpability in crimes committed against these United States this committee is seeking to establish?

FULSOME. Are we speaking of the guilt of that culpability?

THE CHAIR. We are, sir.

FULSOME. Then, yes, sir, I was. Not in the matter of being guilty, but rather yes, I did serve as a member.

THE CHAIR. According to the files you have provided us, you functioned in a good many roles?

FULSOME. Providing those files have been no further tampered with, I did, yes, sir.

THE CHAIR. You did, at one time, act as a spy, did you not?

FULSOME. It was my covert pleasure to do that, yes, sir.

THE CHAIR. You were a member of the Secretive Service?

FULSOME. Being a spy was merely my cover, yes, sir. Since the outing of CIA operative, Valerie Plame, a dozen years ago by someone in the former administration who has yet to be named, let alone confessed or prosecuted, it has become more and less common knowledge that anyone who was everyone was a spy in those days, Mister Chairman.

THE CHAIR. I'd like, if you would, tell the committee what exactly the nature of your duties were during the period in my last reference. Or shall we save time and have you tell us that, to the best of your ability, you just can't recall?

FULSOME. I pride myself, Mister Chairman, on having no problem whatsoever in ever recalling each and every minutia, real or imagined, that might in any way threaten the security of the very best America in the world, sir.

THE CHAIR. Then you are that rarest of men, Mister Fulsome: a committee witness who doesn't have to look at his driver's license to help him remember what his own name is.

FULSOME. In parry your query, sir, chief among my former duties in the former administration was to act as assistant aide to the acting adviser of the deputy head of the Center for Shame and Public Apology.

THE CHAIR. That was, I believe, a think tank, was it not?

FULSOME. We all thought so, yes, sir.

THE CHAIR. And what is it do you think it was that you all thought about?

FULSOME. I would have to say that majorly among our priorities was the creation of scenarios to promote and foist the image of the former president as being capable of delivering not only sound bites but sound policy, as well. That, in any case, was my first and primordial role as a director of POOP, sir.

THE CHAIR. POOP?

FULSOME. Our Photo Op Operations Program.

THE CHAIR. Would that be yet another operation that Congress overlooked in our oversight?

FULSOME. Our activities were pretty hard to track, Mister Chairman. It was part of our mission to fly below the radar in making as sure as we could that our even-then defunct-seeming commander-in-chief was always seen in the best, the most positive light imaginable. Especially whenever he finally managed to rush into one catastrophic situation or another, so often so tardy we once thought of having him show up with a note from his mother.

THE CHAIR. Catastrophes? Are we talking floods and flus, to name a few?

FULSOME. If I might explain what I mean before I answer that, sir?

THE CHAIR. Any order will do.

FULSOME. For the purpose of the President's re-electability chances to not only serve but to survive a second term, it was determined that our best bet right off the bat was to take a page out of England's Sir Winston Churchill's play book, sir, and to do everything we could to turn the president into the image of a wartime leader.

THE CHAIR. The first step of which would be the necessity of providing him with a war.

FULSOME. Those details were left to others to see to, Mister Chairman. Others who had done that sort of thing before. Others who were itching to do that sort of thing again. Our job was to project a leader with an even more fearful personality than the one the American people had come to accept. Watching the president acting from the depths of his intellect, plus the measured pace with which he responded to chaotic events other than those which he himself had created, we soon realized that what we had on our hands was a chief executive with the unlimited potential for becoming known as a disastrous president, as well.

THE CHAIR. And the result of that realization was what?

FULSOME. A modus operandi, sir. That, and the subsequent issuance of an M.O. memo. Our first priority in any emergency which qualified for Oval Office attention – one that met the minimum requirement of at least four figures in casualties – was to immediately jump start the president's sincerity. Be it a tsunami, a quake, or any one of your pandemics, my people were immediately dispatched to wherever the president might be vacationing at the moment, make sure his shirtsleeves were rolled up to the approved level to signify he'd been informed of whatever the latest calamity when he was right in the middle of his working hour –

THE CHAIR. And then you swung into action?

FULSOME. Yes, sir. Starting with drawing straws to see which of us was going to have to tell the president that he was going to have to swing into action.

THE CHAIR. The president did not like hearing bad news.

FULSOME. This is a president who prefers creating it. That way, he feels he's got a better chance of knowing how something got started.

THE CHAIR. Is it true, Mister Fulsome, as part of the testimony you offered at the former president's impeachment proceedings, that one of your duties was to produce an assemblage, a DVD of news footage that would give him some idea of any disaster that did not go away in 24 hours or less?

FULSOME. The president hates disasters. Despite his talent for them.

THE CHAIR. Hence, these DVDs?

FULSOME. It was my job to load them into the monitor on the president's stationary bike inside the War Room.

THE CHAIR. This was a multi-tasking president.

FULSOME. Always give a busy man something he can assign other people to do, that's what he always used to say, yes, sir.

THE CHAIR. And his reaction, once the president understood the magnitude of one or another of these calamities that marked the wonderful times he always asserted the country was going through?

FULSOME. Allowing him a week to ten days to digest the impact of what he had watched to sink in, the president was then handed a standardized speech. This would be a prepackaged set of platitudinous promises and pledges, laced with the appropriate empathy. In addition, for blame-shifting purposes, he was also given a list of names, other than his own, who could be held responsible for what had happened, as well as a multiple choice of explanations for how long it had taken for him to do whatever it was that he was about to do, no matter how many untold billions might have to be spent, or how many untold further taxes might have to be cut. The speech served as the basis for a prime time address to the nation by the president – after the president was primed as to which nation it was he was addressing.

THE CHAIR. And from there?

FULSOME. From there, the former First Lady and the former First Pet on his arm, the president would stride to the Marine chopper parked on the White House lawn, strap himself into his stationary bike, and off he went to wherever the L.Z.D. – the Latest Zone of Devastation was.

THE CHAIR. And you accompanied the president all through this?

FULSOME. The Photo Op Unit followed in our own plane, sir.

THE CHAIR. Your own plane.

FULSOME. The W.C., sir.

THE CHAIR. The W.C.?

FULSOME. The wigs and costumes plane.

THE CHAIR. Wigs and – ?

FULSOME. Those that were to be worn by the members of my unit, yes, sir.

THE CHAIR. What in God's name are we talking about? What sort of wigs? What kind of costumes?

FULSOME. Anything, Mister Chairman, say from firefighters' gear to construction workers' hard hats and tool belts to armed forces members of any and all services and sexes' uniforms.

THE CHAIR. And each with an appropriate hairdo?

FULSOME. It takes a Village People, Mister Chairman. We also traveled with a supply of beer-stained coveralls and sweat-caked baseball caps in the event that we had to portray those of the trailer trash persuasion. Likewise, we were prepared, if necessary, to pass for grief-stricken farmers or sharecroppers who had lost their livestock and/or their families, thanks to flood or fire, or any other "F" word that might fit the bill.

THE CHAIR. Your assignment was to "portray" these people? These farmers or these soldiers? Or any of these other what-have-yous who were suddenly turned into have-nots?

FULSOME. Victors or victims, it was all in a day's work for us, Mister Chairman. After nine-eleven we had to be prepared twenty-five-seven to turn ourselves into background wherever it was the president might have found himself engaged in an impromptu TV press conference that we had previously managed to arrange for him. I should mention that we also traveled with our own set of young Afro-American children.

THE CHAIR. Your own set of – ?

FULSOME. It's not that black youngsters aren't always thick as flies on a plate of brownies wherever tragedy strikes, but not relying on that kind of luck, we always brought a complement of our own along for the president to be photographed smiling at and talking down to. He particularly liked patting the littler one's heads. It was our way of driving home the message that the president was completely at home with other disadvantaged people and that his compassion was in no way color coded.

THE CHAIR. This practice of yours, it never troubled anyone?

FULSOME. Well, we had to take their nap times and school work into consideration, in terms of loading them up.

THE CHAIR. I was referring to the deceitfulness embodied in your entire operation, sir.

FULSOME. Deceitful, sir? Deceitful in the pejorative sense?

THE CHAIR. Deceitful in the sense of dishonest. Deceitful inasmuch as you made it a practice to misconstrue the American people over and over again, never once being whoever it was that you took such great pains to make them think that you were. Didn't any of you think that was terrible?

FULSOME. Terrible times create terrible thinking, Senator. For a time we tried allowing our real life counterparts to act on their own behalfs, but can you imagine how costly and dangerous it is to go around pulling actual troops who are being shot at or possibly even being blown up out of a battle and then having to do a one-eighty and putting them back in harm's way after a photo op? Or to get a child – of any color –to cry when you'd like it to?

THE CHAIR. And was the previous, then-commander-in-chief aware of the routine staging, if the not downright faking of events routine?

FULSOME. I was told by those who were responsible for what he thought that he was only dimly aware, sir.

THE CHAIR. Which was more than less his permanent mode of awareness, thinking about anything at all not being one of his strongest suits.

FULSOME. I daresay action figures far outsell thinking figures, wouldn't you, Mister Chairman?

THE CHAIR. But would you say that, in principle, the president condoned the ongoing charade in which you were so involved in?

FULSOME. In my opinion, I don't really recall, Mister Chairman.

THE CHAIR. You don't recall your own – ?

FULSOME. In the course of my career I've been assigned so many opinions, it's not that easy to remember which ones I might still might be holding onto, sir.

THE CHAIR. Do you by any chance recall assuring this committee that you never had a problem recalling anything whatsoever at all?

FULSOME. I spoke without considering the role that time plays, sir.

THE CHAIR. This was just moments ago.

FULSOME. It was?

THE CHAIR. Not five minutes ago.

FULSOME. That was then, sir. Now is now.

THE CHAIR. Why the reluctance to respond, Mister Fulsome?

FULSOME. If the Chair will allow me a moment to unburden myself?

THE CHAIR. The committee always sets aside a few moments for that purpose.

FULSOME. I would only like to say that what you have opined as my reluctance is more an expression of a conviction, sir. A conviction that prior to each of their individual impeachments, each of the chief executives which I had the privilege to serve, strove at all times to protect the American people from the firestorm of unwarranted ill will of which this nation is the chief recipient. This constant piling on of charges by the present administration strikes me as grossly unfair to two formerly courageous men, whose every effort and only crime was their unstinting dedication to the security of this nation against a vast host of countless dangers, regardless of how many of them they themselves may have inspired. I thank the committee for affording me the opportunity to amplify myself.

THE CHAIR. Thank you, Mister Fulsome.

(Sound: A gavel)

THE VOICE. Exhausting his time with the witness, the Chair then threw the questioning up to other members of the committee.

THE CHAIR. Senator Jordan?

JORDAN. I have a brief statement, if I may Mister Chairman.

THE VOICE. Recently re-elected Senator Rheba Jordan has just begun her third term as defender of the last First Family, which includes the perpetual and still-present governor of her home state of Florida. The senator, whose previous political experience was once serving as a flower girl at the former president's wedding, is wearing a pin-striped three-piece suit by Donatella Versace, topped off by leather and tortoise shell bifocals by Giorgio Armani. Her attaché case is by Alexander McQueen.

JORDAN. In response to the blistering level of attacks with which the witness has so far been battered, it is on the subject of deception, Mister Chairman, into which I wish to wade. When good, patriotic colonials disguised themselves as native American Indians in staging the Boston Tea Party, did one single one of us raise our voice in opposition when that action took place back in 1773? Was it any more deceptive when, just a few, short years later, in 1964, the late, former President Lyndon B. Johnson lied to the American people about the incident in Tonkin Bay, so that he could ratchet up the escalation of the Vietnam conflict into what rightly should and could have been the quagmire to end all quagmires if only we had had the gumption to stay the course? Which, by the way, had he had, we could rightfully, to this day still be fighting over there?

THE CHAIR. The Chair –

JORDAN. Better a deception for me, any time, Mister Chairman! Better a deception than a defeat! Better the waffling of a thousand white lies than the waving of a single white flag. Without deception, it is impossible to protect any democracy that is based on truthfulness in government. I, for one if no other, salute the witness, Mister Chairman. I salute him for doing all that his country called upon him to do. I salute him for answering that call with a totally blind, unquestioning and purposeful single mindlessness.

FULSOME. I only did whatever I was told to believe was right, ma'am.

JORDAN. For which I have not one flotilla of doubt.

THE CHAIR. If the senator has reached the end of her briefness?

JORDAN. Thank you, Mister Chairman.

THE CHAIR. You have no other speeches masquerading as questions?

JORDAN. I never know, Mister Chairman.

(Sound: A gavel)

THE CHAIR. The witness is excused.

FULSOME. From your lips, Mister Chairman.

THE VOICE. After a short recess which allowed committee members to vote to repeal the previous administration's amendment authorizing the phrase, "The Holy Ghost," to be included as part of the Pledge of Allegiance, the hearings were once again resumed.

(Sound: A gavel)

UPCHUCK. The committee will please come to order.

(Sound: A gavel)

THE VOICE. Sitting in as chairman was the long ranking majority member Senator Stuart Upchuck, the chair having flown to the ceremonies celebrating the present administration's renewed commitment to the Kyoto Treaty, whose environmental warnings were for so long ignored and denounced by the previous administration. The ceremonies are scheduled to begin later today in the Niagara Desert, in the city of Buffalo, New York.

(Sound: A gavel)

UPCHUCK. Thank you.

THE VOICE. Wyoming's senior senator, Senator Samuel Upchuck has been in the U.S. upper chamber for twenty-seven consecutive terms, including the five which he spent while in ICU in a total vegetative state.

UPCHUCK. Will the witness please give his name for the record for this and any possible future hearings?

WITNESS. I'll do the best I can, Senator. My name is highly classified, sir. My actual name.

UPCHUCK. You are clueless as to your own - youness?

WITNESS. Yes, sir.

UPCHUCK. Don't you ever have any curiosity about who you might be?

WITNESS. Or who I ever might have been, for that matter, sir.

UPCHUCK. You weren't ever tempted to sneak a look at your mail?

WITNESS. Under the provisions of the repealed Patriot Act Seventeen, there were always others who were always glad to do that for me.

UPCHUCK. Surely with the old administration out of power you've been able to get your own name back.

WITNESS. There's a six month wait for names, sir. In the meantime, the FBI has given me a loaner.

UPCHUCK. A John Doe.

WITNESS. A John Done, actually. They ran out of Doe's some time ago.

UPCHUCK. You did, however, serve in one or more of the foregone administration's agencies, did you not? Surely, that much you're allowed to tell us?

DONE. I'm prepared to bite the buckshot, sir.

UPCHUCK. Would chief among those agencies be the Office of Denying Information regarding Our United States?

DONE. I was chief officer of ODIOUS, yes, sir.

UPCHUCK. Whose mission, would I be correct, in even half ascertaining, was to help keep the American people in as much of the dark as possible?

DONE. If blindness is good enough for justice, Senator, we saw no reason to keep the American people otherwise.

UPCHUCK. I would like to go over a short selection of some of the information which your agency saw fit to withhold from the public.

DONE. Yes, sir.

UPCHUCK. Let us start with the former vice president.

DONE. If you will just give me a moment to remember how to tremble, sir.

UPCHUCK. In the period before his, the vice president's impeachment, which followed on the heels of the impeachment of the president who preceded him, was your agency ever the least bit honest with the American people all over this country about the true state of the first ex Vice, who then went on to become the next ex-president's health, Mister Done?

DONE. The truth is, the ex-vice president-slash-ex-president did not have one extra scrap of health to spare, sir.

UPCHUCK. He was sicker than we knew?

DONE. It is my belief that no one then any more than anyone now has ever properly gauged just how really sick the ex-Chief and co-Chief Executive really was, sir.

UPCHUCK. Would you venture to hazard a guess on your own, now that it's safe to?

DONE. Mainly, I believe, going by what were considered facts during that period, that it all had to do with the man's heart, Senator.

UPCHUCK. That much was more or less known from what we were persistently misinformed about through the press.

DONE. What was much less known than more was that, in the opinion of those who went around in the best medical circles, in all probability, the root cause of Mister Cheney's problem was congenital.

UPCHUCK. I thought you said it was his heart.

DONE. What it was was it was discovered at his birth that the heart that he'd been born with was in fact an artificial one.

UPCHUCK. He was born with an artificial heart?

DONE. Heartlessness runs in the Cheney family, yes, sir. For years, doctors tried without success to find him an actual, human heart as a replacement.

UPCHUCK. A transplant?

DONE. Yes, sir. One sufficiently small enough to fit inside Mister Cheney's cavity, one that might survive such a hostile environment.

UPCHUCK. Without success?

DONE. Over the years, what passed for his heart routinely rejected anything remotely resembling a real one.

UPCHUCK. Aortically challenged as he was, one would have thought he would have championed stem cell research, would he not have? Instead of fighting it so tooth and nail as he continued to do?

DONE. The vice president was much more interested in cells of a prison nature than in those that had to do with stems.

UPCHUCK. He was, of course, famous for being equally tooth and nail pro-torture.

DONE. Yes, sir.

UPCHUCK. As evidenced by his long and devoted marriage to a real life Iron Maiden.

DEBRITUS. Mister Chairman?

THE CHAIR. The Chair recognizes the gentle lady from Georgia.

THE VOICE. Famous in the Senate Cloak Room for her sharp tongue, Senator Deborah Debritus formerly served two lengthy periods as director of the FBA – the Federal Bureau of Attitude.

DEBRITUS. Thank you, Mister Chairman. I find myself fighting the clock, due as I am to answer charges of perjury this morning before the House Bankruptcy Committee regarding my reputed role in the previous administration's Chinese money laundering scandal. I would like to do more than just skim beneath the surface with this witness, Mister Chairman – As I fear, because of his past ties, Mister Done faces being branded here today with a very broad brush indeed. On the subject, for instance, of stem cell research, there was a reason, a very sound, practical reason did there not happen to be, Mister Done, for those of us of the ancedental administration to offer such stiff resistance to it?

DONE. There was, indeed, Madam Senator.

DEBRITUS. And in the deposition that you gave before this committee, can you remember anything you said that was the truth regarding this subject?

DONE. I said quite simply that there was no way in the world that anyone could ever predict with any degree of certainty that any single transplanted cell might not in fact bear the same sexual orientation as the donor of that pre-referenced cell.

DEBRITUS. Meaning?

DONE. Meaning that, at the end of the day, no one could ever guarantee that a heterosexual recipient would not be in danger of receiving a fragment of a homosexual cell if the donor of that cell was himself similarly disoriented.

DEBRITUS. The introduction of such a rogue component might have the potential for quite possibly wiping out a straight man's hard drive? Is that a fair hypothesis of your apprehension, sir?

DONE. Some homosexuals themselves, and I personally can't think of a better grouping for them, haven't they on their own bat made the case for their abominable aberration being genetic in nature?

DEBRITUS. I've read that, too, although I have many doubts with it.

DONE. Whether they are born with the deviation or it just being a matter of an acquired taste, let those who are afflicted of it keep whatever it is they've got stuffed deep down inside their genes, that's what I've always said.

DEBRITUS. You are, of course, aware of how we, in the days when we constituted the majority, how we were so viciously reviled against for how verbally pro we were in being anti-same-sex marriage?

DONE. There was no one antier on subject than I was, ma'am. For which, I got a pretty good dose of that community's revilement, I might add, a form of harassment that was way up close and personal.

DEBRITUS. Providing it's possibly much too graphic, I'm certain the committee would be more than willing to share that harassment with us.

DONE. I just hope that not one of your members ever wakes up, as I did out of a deep sleep one night, to see a mob of men decked out in hoods and purple robes, going about burning a giant phallus on any of their front lawns.

DEBRITUS. I trust that none of your children were exposed to that.

DONE. Fortunately, my little boys had been invited to a sleep over date at our priest's house. If I may add a postscript – I'd like to add that their tactics did not in any way dissuade me from continuing to fight the good fight. That their crowd did not alter by one lick or a single iota my firm belief that if the good Lord had meant for two men to lie down one on top of the other – May I be blunt, Madam Senator?

DEBRITUS. You may be as unminced as you like, Mister Done.

DONE. Only to say that if it was meant for two men to lie down one on top of the other, the good Lord would have given at least one of them a vagina.

DEBRITUS. Beautifully put, sir.

DONE. I might add that I feel equally the same way about lesbians, ma'am. And that is in spite of the many charges that those among that group have leveled up against me, with their constant accusations of me as being guilty of anti-feminism.

WOMAN'S VOICE. *(Shouts):* Death to bigots!

UPCHUCK. Order!

(Sound: Tumult in the room)

WOMAN'S VOICE. Death to bigots!

(Sound: A gavel)

THE CHAIR. We will have no –

(Sound: Added tumult)

THE CHAIR. We will have no order here, please. That woman must be removed.

(Sound: A gavel)

(Crowd settling down)

THE VOICE. The protester, taken into custody, was later diagnosed as suffering from a severe case of PBS.

THE CHAIR. Order.

THE VOICE. *(finishing)* Post Bush Syndrome. The drug industry, which has been cut back to making jillions instead of the gazillions they reaped during the previous administration, has yet to produce an antidote for the this illness, which has stricken untold numbers, including some who, as yet unborn, are already deep in debt because of the rolling tax cuts made at the time of their conception.

(Sound: A gavel)

THE VOICE. The Acting Chairman, somewhat in disarray over the frazzlement created by the outburst, adjourned the committee for the Fourth of July weekend, scheduling their next session for the week before Christmas or the tenth anniversary of the trial of Saddam Hussein, whichever came first.

(Sound: (A gavel)

THE CHAIR. For its first order of business on the resumption of its hearings into the abrogation of the previous administration, the committee would like to take a closer look at size of the morass which our military was thrown into. To supply the committee along those lines, I call, as our next witness – Lance Corporal Eduardo Diaz.

DIAZ. Present and accounted for, sir.

THE CHAIR. You are a member of the Fifth Battalion of the Seventh Cavalry, Corporal?

DIAZ. That is my unit, sir, although I am on temporary assignation to Walter Reed Hospital, here in Washington, D.C., sir.

THE CHAIR. Temporary?

DIAZ. Until it is decided whether either I or the hospital is to be moved to a different location, sir.

THE CHAIR. Walter Reed was in fact at one time past closed down by the past administration, was it not?

DIAZ. No one expected the never ending flow of wounded, sir. No one ever budgeted for so many bodies.

THE CHAIR. I gather this is the first time you have ever appeared before an investigating committee before?

DIAZ. This is my maiden tour, yes, sir. I have no priors.

THE CHAIR. There are certain protocols that are required to be observed here, Corporal.

DIAZ. Whatever they are, you just have to give me the order, sir. It's not even necessary for me to understand it,

THE CHAIR. I appreciate that, Corporal Diaz. To begin with, a witness must stand when first addressing the chair.

DIAZ. I know that, sir.

THE CHAIR. Then why –?

DIAZ. I don't have any legs, sir.

THE CHAIR. I see.

DIAZ. If I could, I'd be happy to stand here for a week, sir.

THE CHAIR. How it is being the case, you may sit, Corporal. We can just skip over the standing up part and go right to you taking the oath.

DIAZ. I would appreciate that, sir.

THE CHAIR. Never let it be said, I always say.

DIAZ. Yes, sir.

THE CHAIR. Please raise your right hand, if you would.

DIAZ. I don't have one of those either, sir.

THE CHAIR. Oh. Of course.

DIAZ. Actually, I do have one, sir, but it's in the shop.

THE CHAIR. I must say, I would have thought that you'd been a bit better prepared for your appearance today, Corporal. You've known you were going to be here for over a month now.

DIAZ. I can raise my left hook, sir, if that'd be okay with the committee.

THE CHAIR. I guess that'll have to do, if that's all you're able to raise at the moment.

DIAZ. I'd say that's pretty much the long and short of it, sir.

PROCTOR. Mister Chairman?

THE CHAIR. Senator Proctor?

PROCTOR. May I suggest to my distinguished colleague that, in view of the witness' demonstrated willingness to sacrifice a multiplicity of his life and limbs in the service of his country, that the committee show some forbearance in the matter of his being sworn in and not require him to do so at all?

THE CHAIR. Let me put it to the members of the committee that, in lieu of a gratuitous and possibly insensitive show of hands, if all those in favor of Senator Proctor's suggestion would simply say –

ALL. Aye.

THE CHAIR. The vote being all ayes, the witness may consider himself forsworn.

DIAZ. Thank you, Mister Chairman.

THE CHAIR. I understand, Corporal that you would like to begin by reading a personal statement to the committee?

DIAZ. I understand that, as well, yes, sir.

THE CHAIR. You may read when ready, then.

DIAZ. Thank you, sir. *(Clears his throat, reads)* "By way of background, let me say that I was originally born on February 25, 1985, BF."

THE CHAIR. BF?

DIAZ. Before the Fence.

THE CHAIR. Your place of birth being?

DIAZ. The city of Cuernavaca, sir, which is located just one republic south of this republic in the Republic of Mexico.

THE CHAIR. You are not an American by birth?

DIAZ. More by stealth, sir.

THE CHAIR. Stealth.

DIAZ. I was two months old when my father smuggled me across the border.

THE CHAIR. On his own person?

DIAZ. In his toilet kit.

THE CHAIR. You were born to illegal immigrants.

DIAZ. Third generation, Mister Chairman. For over fifty years, the Diaz family has been swimming up the Rio Grande to get to this country come hell or high water, sir. I have loved America and all that it stands for since I was old enough to hide. After the invasion of Iraq for any one of the many reasons that we were given for why we had to do it, I made the decision that by joining the army I could in my own way repay my adopted land for some of what it's allowed me do for it. I was also aware that fighting for the red, white and blue was the quickest way for a brown man to get a green card.

THE CHAIR. *(Silence, then)* Is that the end of your statement, Corporal?

DIAZ. There's no more on the paper, sir.

THE CHAIR. You did, of course, receive a bonus for enlisting in the armed forces?

DIAZ. Most of which I sent it to my relatives in Mexico so that they, too, could make a better life for themselves.

THE CHAIR. Money for their educations.

DIAZ. Or for swimming lessons, whichever.

THE CHAIR. Taking it from there then, after you enlisted, can you tell us what happened next?

DIAZ. After I enlisted.

THE CHAIR. After you enlisted.

DIAZ. Yes, sir. Right after I enlisted, I volunteered.

THE CHAIR. To go overseas?

DIAZ. To stay in the army longer.

THE CHAIR. I'm not sure I understand.

DIAZ. What happened was, a recruiting officer got me to re-up on the way to where I parked my car when I went in to enlist. Next thing I knew, I found myself in the thick of the hot stuff.

THE CHAIR. You went right into battle?

DIAZ. No, sir, right into pastry school.

THE CHAIR. Pastry school?

DIAZ. Armed Forces pastry school, sir. I was assigned to the crack 82nd Airborne Bakers' Battalion. The 82nd was the cream of the crop, sir. Its motto is: "They also serve those who dish up and serve."

THE CHAIR. That was the unit with which you were attached in Iraq?

DIAZ. It was, yes, sir.

THE CHAIR. And it was there that you were assigned to duty in the prisoner of war prison at Abu Ghraib?

DIAZ. We were told to consider it a detainee holding area, sir.

THE CHAIR. Can you tell the committee what exactly the difference is between someone who is a detainee and somebody who is a prisoner of war?

DIAZ. That's what we all said, sir. As far as the holding part, I wouldn't put my arms around one of 'em for five dollars.

THE CHAIR. And your duties at Abu Ghraib consisted of what exactly what, can you tell us?

DIAZ. Well, in my eighth tour of what was supposed to be just really the one only, it was mostly supposed to be kitchen duty, sir, helping prepare meals for the prison personnel, like the ones on guard and the eats for the detainees. Abu Grub, we called it.

THE CHAIR. They each received the same – ?

DIAZ. *(Adding)* And for the dogs, too. The dogs and the guards got the same rations, if that's what you were asking, sir. Plus which the dogs might've got a extra chunk of detainee once in a while when one of their handlers let 'em get a little too close.

THE CHAIR. The dogs were allowed to bite a detainee?

DIAZ. Only if the detainee bit the dog first, sir.

THE CHAIR. This was what you did at the beginning, is that what you said?

DIAZ. Yes, sir, before.

THE CHAIR. Before what?

DIAZ. Before the kitchen staff got reassigned on account'a the strike.

THE CHAIR. Some sort of military strike?

DIAZ. Not exactly, sir. In protest against their being water boarded or electrified so often by our interrogators, as well as sometimes having some of their privates twisted by some of our privates, the prisoners just upped and stopped eating their meals after a while.

THE CHAIR. So we're talking about a prisoners' strike.

DIAZ. Yes, sir. Eventually, there being less people to prepare for due to the torture protest, plus which so much of our electricity being used on one testicle or another, I wasn't all that needed after a while to help with the food anymore.

THE CHAIR. And so you were assigned to different duties?

DIAZ. Yes, sir.

THE CHAIR. Rather than helping with the food.

DIAZ. Yes, sir.

THE CHAIR. And those would be what?

DIAZ. I was told to help with the torture. It was like starting all over, sir. Learning new skills, and all. I had to start, more or less, at the bottoms.

THE CHAIR. The bottoms?

DIAZ. Of the detainees, sir. Arranging all their butts, stacking 'em one on top of the other. Smearing 'em with feces. Sometimes I felt like I was back in baker's school.

THE CHAIR. How big of a problem did you have with that? Were you able to ignore the fact that you'd been ordered to torture prisoners? That torture itself was illegal?

DIAZ. We were told to think of it as humiliation. Which was pretty much how we all felt about it, anyway.

THE CHAIR. And so you had no problem with these new "duties" to which you'd been assigned?

DIAZ. Well, the hours were longer, and there were all those reports that had to prepare and shred at the end of the day –

THE CHAIR. You had no moral problem with that?

DIAZ. None of us in that group had all that much time to walk around with any of those on our mind, no, sir.

THE CHAIR. Tell me, Corporal - in this only-for humiliation- military-group in which you found yourself in –

DIAZ. It was only half-military, sir. About the rest of the other half were mainly civilian contractors.

THE CHAIR. You worked together?

DIAZ. Hand in glove, sir. Although that was not a particularly too good of a situation, really.

THE CHAIR. In what way?

DIAZ. Well, those guys, those civilians, they were getting paid a whole lot of money, y'know what I mean, for what they were doing?

THE CHAIR. For humiliating the detainees?

DIAZ. Yes, sir.

THE CHAIR. Whereas the troops – ?

DIAZ. We had to do it for free. For the others such as myself, it was just more orders to follow. We got our salaries, of course, but we didn't get one penny extra for our humiliation. There was never any sort of bonus or anything. We just did what we did for the flag. All we got out of it was the glory.

THE CHAIR. Tell me, Corporal. About your fellow and sister soldiers that were engaged in these practices –

DIAZ. Our group.

THE CHAIR. Yes.

DIAZ. We were called the Group Using Legally Abusive Guidelines, sir.

THE CHAIR. The Group Using –

DIAZ. GULAG, sir.

THE CHAIR. I see, yes.

DIAZ. You take the first letter of each word, and you –

THE CHAIR. I get it. I promise you, I get it. Tell me, did it ever cross any of your minds that if ever any of you had the misfortune of being captured by the enemy, that you might be subjected to the same treatment you were meting out to others?

DIAZ. Given my condition or pretty much my total lack of one, I never thought there'd have been a whole lot of me for the enemy to torture, sir.

THE CHAIR. In terms of delicacy, would I be going out on a limb if I asked you how it happened that you came to lose so many of your own?

DIAZ. Humvee rolled over me, sir.

THE CHAIR. Good lord.

DIAZ. I was trapped inside. Nine-tenths of my body got crushed.

THE CHAIR. Roadside explosion? Ambush?

DIAZ. No, sir. It happened the night of my high school prom, sir.

THE CHAIR. When you were still a civilian?

DIAZ. Yes, sir.

THE CHAIR. This was an accident that occurred before you joined the army?

DIAZ. Three months before, yes, sir.

THE CHAIR. Are we to understand that the condition in which you are now in, is the same condition in which you were in when the army allowed you to enlist?

DIAZ. They didn't do me any special favors, sir. Whatever was left of me passed my physical with flying colors. Truth be told, the love I have for America being what it is, I would have joined up even if I still had every one of my old bits and pieces, sir.

THE CHAIR. Even though we now have inconvertible proof that the administration then in charge lied, if not its legs, then certainly its head off, in its effort to steam-roll this nation into a war that has wrecked not only havoc but pretty much all of our economy, as well?

DIAZ. To be honest, sir, I myself did a fair share of lying to get into this nation.

THE CHAIR. Allow me to say this, Lance Corporal Eduardo Diaz: You are one fine young man.

DIAZ. Thank you, Senator.

THE CHAIR. To be in your presence is to know that this country could use a lot more men like you, sir.

DIAZ. This country used to have a lot more men like me, sir.

THE VOICE. Before showing highlights of the final day of the hearings, here is a schedule of the coverage of the literature spawned and inspired by the previous administration being presented by AGN's sister channel, ASN, the All Scandal Network. At noon, former Secretary of Defense, Donald Rumsfeld, will discuss his best-selling "Book of Revelations." Mister Rumsfeld will also glibly answer any call-in questions from his cell in United States Penitentiary, in Leavenworth, Kansas — where, after being found guilty of committing preemptive war crimes, Mister Rumsfeld is now serving life for having robbed so many innocent people of their own. Then, at one, ASN plays host to the former chief advisor to the former chief executive, Karl Rove. Often referred to as "Turd Blossom" by the previous occupant of the Oval Office, Mister Rove has written a book devoted to his extremely arch conservative principles, one which he has titled: "First Turd on the Right." Now, for the conclusion of the Abrogate hearings, which opened with the testimony of the committee's last three – three, no less – witnesses.

(Sound: A gavel struck three times)

THE CHAIR. Thank you. Thank you. If we may have a little order, please. Thank you. Madam Former Secretary of State, Condoleezza Rice?

RICE. Mister Chairman.

THE CHAIR. Former First Second Lady, Lynne Cheney?

CHENEY. Mister Chairman.

THE CHAIR. And former Queen Mother, Barbara Bush, the First?

BUSH. You may all sit.

THE CHAIR. Thank you, ma'am.

BUSH. Do call me Barb.

THE CHAIR. Barb?

BUSH. Barb. As in wire.

THE CHAIR. As you are no doubt aware, if any of the witnesses so chooses, the option of making an opening statement is all yours.

BUSH. Thank you, Mister Chairman. I believe we so opt to. Ladies.

(Sound: A pitch pipe)

BUSH. Double, double –

CHENEY. Toil and trouble.

BUSH & CHENEY. Fire burn –

RICE. And caldron bubble.

THE THREE. Double, double toil and trouble, Fire burn and caldron bubble.

(Sound: The gavel)

THE CHAIR. How now, you secret, black, and midnight hags? What is it you do?

WOMEN. Scale of Dragon, Tooth of Wolf, Witches –

BUSH. Mummy,

CHENEY. Maw,

RICE. And Gulf.

UPCHUCK. Gulf? Did she say Gulf, Mister Chairman?

RICE. Gulf Two, Senator. I was too young to stay up and watch the first one.

UPCHUCK. How fulfilled you must feel, being finally able to help start a Gulf War that is all your own.

RICE. I'm not a lawyer, Mister Chairman, or I would surely object to that, sir.

THE CHAIR. You still maintain, do you, Madam Former Secretary of State, that you took no part whatever in the misleadership that led us into going to war against Iraq?

RICE. How many years must I go on denying that I did, sir, before we can both accept that I am telling the truth?

CHENEY. El achbar kahan a moment, if I might, Mister Chairman?

THE CHAIR. Pardon?

HUGHES. It's Arabic, sir. A language I studied the better to facilitate our interference in the region. As to our invasion of Iraq, I should think it would be more than finally clear after all this time that the

CHENEY. Purpose of our mission was so that we could outsource our freedom.

RICE. After nine-eleven, it certainly became far too expensive to maintain it in America. Do you have any idea what it costs to tap just one single phone, Mister Chairman, let alone several millions of them?

THE CHAIR. I am well aware of the metrics of eavesdropping, Madam Witness. I was in Washington long before you took your first cocktail lounge piano lesson.

UPCHUCK. May I also interject my own el achbar whatever-that-was a moment here ago, Mister Chairman? I would just like to hear from whoever will finally tell me why there was such a clamor, such a headlong rush for the topplement of Saddam Hussein's regime, when everyone agreed that it was the Al Quedas who had perpetrated the actual nine-eleven attack that was launched against us?

BUSH. Osama Ben Bama didn't try to kill my boy's daddy, Senator. Or were you out that day? In my family, we don't take kindly to that kind of rudeness.

UPCHUCK. And to how many deaths would you reckon the count must rise, Ma'am, before this country is finally avenged for a death that never once even ever occurred?

BUSH. Better a thousand widows whose faces I have never seen, Senator, than the one that looks out of the mirror at me when I'm doing my daily preen.

UPCHUCK. Does it give you some sort of satisfaction then, to know that the war that never should have started is one that has proved impossible to bring to a stop?

RICE. Still preaching premature withdrawal, Senator?

CHENEY. Americans don't cut and run.

RICE. Only certain, decorated "heroes" do that.

UPCHUCK. Premature?

CHENEY. Would you have had Americans pulling out of this country during the Revolutionary War?

UPCHUCK. After ten years? The hole that you and your Vulcans dug for this country is one that's proved exceedingly difficult to crawl out of.

BUSH. The hole that you and your colleagues voted for because someone held a gun to your heads, Senator?

UPCHUCK. We gave the president the authority to go to war without knowing the true facts.

RICE. You were privy to exactly the same intelligence that the president had.

THE CHAIR. I beg to differ. For possibly the one and only time in his life, the president had more intelligence than anybody.

BUSH. So easy to kick a uniter when he's down, isn't it?

PROCTOR. Was the war honestly all that horrorifical to you, Mister Chairman, or are you now finding it as hard to turn your back on all of that oil as we were once so reluctant to?

THE CHAIR. And at what price, sir? Did you ever in your wildest dreams imagine how many bodies it would cost this country per gallon?

CHENEY. Can we finally not put that liberal, oppositional canard to bed? We were not simply there for the oil.

BUSH. Bully for you, girl.

RICE. We were there to stamp out terror.

CHENEY. Absolutely.

THE CHAIR. But there was no terror until we got there.

UPCHUCK. Finally, a mission accomplished that truly was one.

BUSH. No terror? No terror? If Saddam Hussein had had his way, my son would have long been half an orphan.

THE CHAIR. I, for one, have had my fill of talk of terror.

RICE. Terror has a long shelf life, Senator.

THE CHAIR. Two consecutive terms of fear were quite enough for me, thank you.

BUSH. I taught each of my children the meaning of terror. My husband, too, if the truth be told.

THE CHAIR. Then it's to you that the whole world will never be grateful enough, madam.

BUSH. I should hope not.

THE VOICE. The entire room fell silent by the request-slash-command then issued by the former First Lady-in-Her-Own-Right-slash-Former-First-Mother-In-Law-full-stop.

BUSH. With or without the Chair's permission, Mister Chairman, I have a brief but compelling statement I would like to make regarding these so-called hearings, which it distresses us to say, rather than concentrating on the positive apspects of the past, seem bent on being predominably negative if not downright condemntorial. I will never forget the night that I bore the son who was to become the future, and then later, the past president of these United States.

RICE. A little background music, if it pleases the Chair, Mister Chairman?

THE CHAIR. Without objection.

(**RICE** *and* **CHENEY** *begin softly humming,* "The Battle Hymn of the Republic," *under:*)

BUSH. I remember that night just as clearly as I remember the night on which the second of my former presidents was conceived because I was all alone at the time. Completely alone. As alone as I generally am when my husband is right there beside me. But even he was truly not there that night, having been called away to attend an emergency duck hunt. All alone, I was in the stables, mucking out a manger, when I felt this sudden hot surge, this sensation in my loins. Sensations that were a whole lot more maternal than they were in any way carnal, which really surprised me, since the last time George 41 and I engaged in anything of that nature was back in '46, when we celebrated the Republican takeover of both houses of Congress. But sure enough, nine months later, there we were, the proud mother of a brand new baby boy. His little legs bowed right from the get-go, a little dimple in his smirk, his tiny eyes already starting to bead, we decided to christen him George W. After the country's first president, of course. There was just something about him even then that gave us the feeling that he might turn out to be the country's last.

(**RICE** *and* **CHENEY** *stop humming.*)

BUSH. There were whispers about him from the very beginning. Whispers and snickers. But that only made me love him all the more. At least with whatever I remember love being all about. Some people thought I took a beautiful little boy and spoiled him rotten. I paid them no mind. To me, he was that way from the day he was born. Beautiful, I mean, of course, not rotten. Privileged? Of course. Entitled? Snug in his smugness? Why not? His daddy's rich, and his ma's good lookin', as the old poem goes. If this committee thinks it's going to make any hay making the case that my son's actions in some way damaged this country, let them remember that whatever he did all over this country, he did out of his love for it.

*(***RICE*** *and* **CHENEY** *begin humming* "Rock of Ages. ")*

BUSH. Much has been made of my son's political base. Of the support of those of the far righteousness. Of his need to appease those who were lucky enough to be born more than just the one time that is given to most of us. Let me assure you, Mister Chairman, that when it came to the American safety of the American people, my son never hesitated for a moment to take that same, base attitude toward everyone. And now, finally, how else will this country choose to honor him for how loyal he was? How, let us finally face it, how royal he was?

(As **RICE** *and* **CHENEY**'*s humming builds:)*

BUSH. You hounded him out of office, refusing to allow him to resign that he might better be impeached. Then, you impeached him. You impeached him twice. Once for each term. You sued him for damages which you claim he cost America, sparing him from having to go to court by accepting his check for ten dollars. Letting him settle for one dollar on the trillion. You exiled him to five years at Berlitz, which sentence could be reduced whenever he learned to speak a proper one in English. You drafted his only daughters and sent them off to Iraq. You drove him back to drinking. In public. What's next? How long will it be before you start coming around with your hammer and nails?

THE VOICE. To this day, not one person who was there can believe what it was they saw next in the hearing room.

BUSH. You are none of you worthy of him. None of you.

THE VOICE. *(Continuing)* As suddenly, mysteriously, the Former First Mother's feet slowly began to leave the floor and she began to rise. She began to ascend.

BUSH. I will take him to a better place. A place to which he has sent so many others. So, so many others.

(Her voice fading)

He is above the law. Above the lawmakers. He is himself the law. Whether in the service. Whether as governor. Whether as president. No one has been ever higher than he has. Reigning from above, he will be then highest that he has ever been before.

*(**RICE** and **CHENEY**: a big finish.)*

(Sound: The gavel)

THE VOICE. The sight of the spectacle so compelling, the Chairman, quickly dismissed the committee. In the forty-eight months filled with the countless nolo contenders and habeas corpii before the hearings were set to be resumed prior to their further postponement, any number of developments befell some of Abrogate's key players. Spokespersons for the former president did, in fact, verify his total disappearance, saying that all he left behind was a mail order flight jacket, fragments of a huge bubble, and the remnants of an irremediable sneer. Out of respect for the former president's ascension, members of his party, for all of the following month, were seen wearing their lapel flags at half mast. Upon learning that his wife, the former Mrs. Cheney, had run off with the former Secretary of State, Condoleezza Rice, trying to find any state that would allow them to become wife and wife, the former vice, as well as president promptly suffered a record seventeenth heart attack. After an unsuccessful attempt to die in a hunting accident, he was fined seven dollars for trying to commit suicide with an outdated license and forbidden by law to ever come closer than ten feet to himself again. The hearings were finally indefinitely postponed when the chairman, after pleading innocent to multiple charges of bribery resigned, and retired to his five hundred thousand acre ranch in Abramoff, New Mexico. In an unrelated corporate scandal, Chief Charles Bull, C.E.O. of Yippeo Casinos, when told the government was willing to return one or more of the United States as settlement for the billions his people have been cheated out of, the chief responded on behalf of each and every Indian when he said, very politely: "No, thanks. They're all yours." For AGN - the All Gate Network - goodnight.

THE END